I0624707

Terror at the Observatory

By Jo Carey

COPYRIGHT

Copyright © 2018 by Jo Carey

All rights reserved. No part of this book may be reproduced in any form or by any means, electronic or mechanical, including photocopying, recording, or by any information storage and retrieval system, without permission in writing from the author except by a reviewer who may quote brief passages in a review.

This is a work of fiction. Names, characters, businesses, places, events and incidents are either the products of the author's imagination or used in a fictitious manner. Any resemblance to actual persons, living or dead, or actual events is purely coincidental.

ISBN 13: 978-1-948716-35-2

CHAPTER ONE

"Dr. Young," he said, while feeling around for his glasses on the night stand.

"This is security. There's been an incident with one of the animals on level 5."

"I'll be right there." Putting on jeans and a t-shirt before pulling his access badge over his head, he made a quick pitstop and threw some cold water on his face hoping that would help him wake up. He was on call 24/7, but this was the first time in months he'd been called out at night.

As he made his way out of his quarters on the second floor of the employee dormitory, he joined a flood of people rushing to the main complex. "What's going on?" he shouted into the crowd. Most of the people around him were astronomers and astrophysicists who worked in the above ground portion of EARS. Chad knew they wouldn't be called in because of an issue with the animals.

"They picked up a signal," someone said as the wave of people surged across the strip of desert that separated the dormitory from the main building. When he got close to the main building, Chad could hear some sort of electronic noise over the speakers. Inside people were standing still and staring upward as though they were looking for the source of the noise.

He maneuvered his way through the living statues and got into the elevator. When he walked out on level 5, he was surprised to hear the same electronic noise as upstairs. Two armed guards were standing in the hallway that led to the animal holding cells. He could hear the roars and growls even over the noise coming from the intercom speakers.

"What happened?" he asked the guard that was standing near the first cell.

"I'm not sure what set them off," the guard said. "Are you Dr. Young?"

"Yeah," Chad said, holding up his badge for the guard to see.

"Follow me." When they reached the pen that held a short-faced bear, Chad saw a body in a security uniform lying outside the cell. The bear was holding the guard's arm and using it to strike the wall. Stepping over the body, Chad went to check the other cages. All of the animals were agitated. Only the cages with the mother scimitar cats and their babies were calm. When he took a closer look, he saw the mother cats were lying with their bodies covering the babies—not calm, protective.

"What is that damn noise?" Chad yelled to the guard.

"I don't know sir. It's been going on for a while now."

"Get someone in the comm room to turn off the speakers in the cages."

The guard pulled out his radio and relayed the request. "Dr. Young, they can't turn it off only in the holding cells. They can turn off the whole floor but then we won't hear any emergency messages."

"Do it. My authorization. We have to calm these animals down."

A few minutes later the noise stopped, but it took hours to get the animals calmed down. The bear that attacked the guard would be closely monitored for several days. The EARS medical team transported the injured guard to ground level where he could be medevacked to a hospital in Boise.

Chad slowly walked up and down the hallway watching the animals as they returned to normal. Well normal for animals that haven't been seen on earth for thousands of years.

It was difficult to assess what's normal for these species since the only information about them comes from the fossil records. Any behavioral details are pure speculation. Dr. Young and his staff could study a modern-day bear and make assumptions about how the Short-Faced bear would behave, but everyone knows what happens when you make assumptions.

The situation was further complicated by the process Dr. Young used to create these animals—a process that incorporates some aspects of cloning along with genetic engineering. It's complicated, and it makes it nearly impossible to define what's normal for one of the reintroduced animals. The program is too new, and they simply don't have enough data to speculate on what the norms will be.

After the incident with the guard, the animals calmed down. Dr. Young spent the rest of the night pacing the hall of the animal enclosures with his assistant, Renee. "Do you know what the noise was that was playing on the intercom?"

"Rumor is they picked up an alien signal. I think they were playing it so everyone could hear," Renee said as she met Dr. Young in the middle of the hallway.

"At least that will keep Hastings and Jenkins off our backs for a while."

"We can hope," she said as they continued their walking vigil.

When the rest of the lab staff arrived for the day, Dr. Young held a meeting to review what happened overnight. They put protocols in place to monitor the animals more closely, and Chad headed home to get some much-needed sleep.

His ringing phone woke him once again. He picked it up off the nightstand. "What now?"

"Chad, it's Renee. Sorry to interrupt your sleep again, but can you come back in. The animals are restless. I'd like your assessment."

Three hours of sleep was not nearly enough. This didn't sound like an emergency, so Chad took time for a quick shower and picked up the largest possible cup of coffee from the cafeteria on his way down to the lab.

Renee and the vet were both in the hallway outside the holding cells.

"I'm not sure what we should do," the vet said. "They just seem agitated."

"Let's meet in my office in an hour," Chad said. "I want to observe them myself."

XXX

"The bears and cats seemed more tense than normal," Chad said. "Is it possible this is just because of the commotion last night? I know I'm not feeling normal at this point."

"You may be right," the vet said. "I didn't see anything that was too concerning."

"I checked on the smaller animals we use in the lab," Renee said. "They all seemed normal to me."

"We really need to get the bears and cats moved to the outside pens where they have natural light, fresh air, and more space," Chad said. "Those pens should be ready this week."

CHAPTER TWO

"You can't be serious. Bigfoot? Really? I'm a reporter, Jon. A real one. A good one. I'm not spending the weekend tramping around the woods with crazy people with guns."

"If they actually find something, this could be your big break, Erin."

"There is zero chance they'll find anything except an excuse to drink beer and hassle the reporter. I've paid my dues, Jon. Send someone else."

"Sorry, kid. I need you to cover this. You know you're the creature queen. You've made a name for yourself with your creature stories. Capitalize on it."

"Is Trey doing the camera work?" she asked.

"No. That's why I'm sending you. You can handle the camera and the onscreen stuff. They will only allow me to send one reporter. Look, I know you think this is beneath you, but this is Idaho. A lot of folks around here know there are strange things in the woods. This piece will get big numbers even if you only cover the hunters." Jon had been the news producer at Channel 8 in Boise for decades. He knew what his audience tuned in for.

"Aren't you concerned about the safety aspect? You're sending me off into the woods with a bunch of armed men."

"Don't play the gender card now, Erin. You're better than that."

She crossed her arms over her chest and heaved a sigh. They both knew she wouldn't refuse the assignment.

"I checked out this group. They're serious about this. You'll be armed with bear spray and a weapon. Think of it as a police ride along without the ride."

Back at her desk in the bullpen, Erin pulled up Jon's email with the details on the upcoming bigfoot hunt. Leaning back in her chair, she sipped coffee and wondered how her career had gone so far off track.

When she was the newest on camera reporter at Channel 8, she was excited to cover any story Jon assigned her. Her first assignments were covering local events like fundraisers for the animal shelter. Her love of animals came through on camera. Positive response from viewers led to her covering local cat and dog shows. When she held a snake at the local reptile show, someone on social media dubbed her Channel 8's creature queen, and the name stuck. Since then, she covered every animal related story on Channel 8 whether it was the arrival of a new snow leopard at the zoo, or community reaction to new laws requiring people to clean up after their pets downtown.

Some of the stories were fluff pieces and some had real hard news components. Erin didn't mind paying her dues, but it was tough to see how this bigfoot story would do anything to further her career as a serious journalist. She needed to think about her future because it was becoming clear that she wasn't going to move forward if she stayed at Channel 8.

CHAPTER THREE

Two weeks later...

When he walked into the conference room, conversation stopped.

"Hello Dr. Young. I believe you know everyone so give us your status report on the Homotheriums as soon as you're ready," said Reingold Hastings, CEO of Hastings International, from the video screen. Chad was flattered when the billionaire owner of Hastings International personally came to Berkeley to recruit him, but he was young and naive then. Hastings offered to fund his research into creating modern versions of previously extinct animals.

Chad pulled up the presentation on his tablet. "As you can see from this graph, our Homotherium program is doing well. Two of our specimens have produced healthy offspring. We now have eight of the scimitar cats here. Our work on the short-faced bear is moving ahead. We've created three of the bears--two male and one female. While we continue our efforts on breeding those two species, we're ramping up our work on the smilod...

Alarms blared, and an automated message came through the speakers. "Containment breach in pens 3 and 7. Please shelter in place until security releases you." The message began to repeat before anyone in the room moved.

"Dr. Young, please go see what's going on?" Lab Director Jenkins said all but pushing Chad out the door. He heard the lock click into place after the door closed behind him. When he reached the elevator, he pushed the button before remembering the elevators shut down in any emergency that set off the alarms. He turned and headed for the stairs. Pens 3 and 7 were part of the external animal habitat. Currently all the scimitars and short-faced bears were housed above ground in specially designed pens. It looked like a cross between a cattle ranch and Jurassic Park.

Pushing open the emergency exit on the surface, Chad could hear gunfire and shouting in the distance. He ran toward the pens. The first pen looked to be intact. He could see the three youngest scimitars huddled together in the back of the pen. Clearly the commotion was disturbing them.

Other than the animals being agitated, Chad didn't see anything wrong until he was nearly run over by two security guards carrying a third covered in blood. "What happened?" he asked.

"Not sure. Animals are attacking," one of the men said as they continued on headed for the main building.

A scimitar roar was followed quickly by screaming and gunfire. Chad pushed forward to an empty Pen 3. A portion of the steel reinforced fencing was lying flat on the ground. These were large animals--the full-grown scimitars weigh 600 pounds, while the short-nosed bears aren't quite as large as their ancestors, but the adults weigh in around 1000 lbs.

Chad was sticking to the pathway that circled all the pens. He started seeing splashes of blood and bits of tissue. Before he reached pen 7, he tripped over something and ended up face down in dirt. "Damn," he said, looking back to see what tripped him up. Lying across the path was a jean-clad leg. He couldn't tell any more than that. He put his hands under his shoulders to lever himself up and realized the sandy soil under his hands was wet and sticky. A closer look confirmed what he already feared--he had fallen into a pool of blood.

It was tough to imagine how things could get worse. When he got close to pen 7, he heard screams and followed the sounds. A section of the fence was lying on the ground. He followed a security guard into the pen.

One of the bears had a white-coated lab tech in its mouth. "Shoot it," Chad yelled to the guard. "What are you waiting for?"

"The way he's twisting her around, I can't get a clear shot at the bear. I don't want to hit her."

As they stood helplessly watching, the bear put the woman on the ground and placed a huge paw in the middle of her back. Chad couldn't tell if she was dead or alive, but he was sure her rib cage was being crushed under the bear's weight.

"Do you have tranquilizer darts?" he asked the guard.

"Yeah. They don't want us to kill the animals," he said.

Before Chad had the chance to say the woman would survive being tranquilized, the bear bit into her upper leg and tore it from her body. Chad turned and vomited into the dirt. The guard just stood as though he was hypnotized. Chad pulled the rifle from the guard's hands and fired tranquilizer darts into the bear until he ran out of ammunition, and the bear fell to the ground.

Chad tugged the guard with him until they were both outside the damaged fence. He pulled out his radio. "This is Dr. Young, have all members of the animal support team meet me at pen 7."

He pulled out his phone and dialed the private number of Director Jenkins. "We need to put together a hunt team. We have bears and scimitar cats loose on the grounds. There are several dead and wounded. I need a team of hunters to recover them." Chad didn't wait for questions. He hung up and turned his attention to those arriving to help.

"There's a tranquilized bear in there with a female staff member. I'm not sure if she's still alive or not. Transport the bear to Level 5 and secure him in one of the holding cells. Once the animal is out of the area, the EMTs can deal with the woman."

After checking the remaining animals in the open-air pens, he headed back inside to talk to the director.

CHAPTER FOUR

Erin walked into the bullpen and dropped her bag on the desk.

"What the heck took so long?" Jon asked. "The police band said they stopped the guy an hour ago."

"They did, but they couldn't get him out of the car."

"Did he crash?"

"No. He was afraid to move."

"You're not going to believe it," Trey, the cameraman said. "I wouldn't believe it if I hadn't been standing right there."

"This sounds good," Jon said. "Go on."

"The stolen car belongs to an exotic pet sitter. She was on her way to return a couple of pets she'd been caring for at her home. Both of them were in cages in the backseat. Behind the driver's seat was a macaw, and behind the passenger seat was a large boa constrictor. The pet sitter ran into the convenience store for a coffee when the perp stole the car.

"Apparently, the macaw's owner is a big Liam Neeson fan. I guess this bird is pretty vocal. One of his favorite lines is 'I will find you, and I will kill you.' He kept repeating it. When the perp looked into the back seat, he saw the snake but heard the Macaw. He was convinced the boa was threatening him."

Jon was laughing so hard he had to wipe tears from his eyes.

"The guy refused to get out of the car. They had to bring the pet sitter over so she could remove the animals. Once they were out of sight, the police were able to take the guy into custody."

"Sounds like one of those stupid criminal stories."

"Whenever animals are involved, it always adds an element of the unexpected," Erin said.

Jo Carey

"Get that footage to editing. We'll air it at 5:30. The creature queen is back," Jon said. "I've got a new assignment for you Erin. Come to my office, when you're ready."

<h2 align="center">XXX</h2>

After Jon explained Erin's new assignment, she asked, "Why me? If EARS really has detected a signal from space, that's big news. Since you're not sending Tiff, you must not believe there's much of a story."

Jon didn't bother to argue the point. "Just cover the story and be happy for the opportunity."

"Fine. I'll tell Trey."

"No Trey. Just video the press conference and do a voice over," Jon said. "I can't afford to invest too much in this."

Erin wasn't surprised, but it still hurt. She'd been an on-camera reporter for the local news station for years but was always passed over for the anchor spot or the lead story. When she chose to pursue a career in television news, she knew it would be an uphill battle. She was more the short, dark-haired, tom-boy type than the leggy blond the station seemed to prefer.

Erin spent a few hours at her desk in the bullpen doing research on EARS, the Earth Array Station, a privately-owned radio telescope array in the southeastern Oregon desert not far from the small town where she grew up.

A few weeks ago, an internet post claimed the observatory detected a signal from space. There had been more reports on social media but nothing official. The invite Jon forwarded about the press conference didn't provide any further clues. Erin felt sure her trip to the observatory would be a waste of time, but at least she could enjoy the drive. She thought maybe some windshield time would help her decide what to do about her career which seemed to be permanently stuck in park.

If EARS did detect a signal, they wouldn't release any details until it had been thoroughly investigated. If any

11

observatory ever picked up an alien communication, Erin knew the American people would learn about it first in a presidential news conference if they ever heard about it at all. With her expectations firmly in check, she made some notes for the story and headed home.

CHAPTER FIVE

"I got your message," Harrison said. "Do you really think EARS called this press conference because they have something they're ready to share or are they trying to quell the rumors? They'd need longer to investigate and have any real facts."

Harrison listened while Joyce, his long-time editor at Science Discovery Magazine, weighed in with her opinion.

"Yeah, I guess you're right. I need to go hear what they have to say. I'll be in touch." He hung up his phone, made travel arrangements, and headed to the bedroom to pack a bag.

Harrison was always skeptical but curious. As a scientist and a reporter, that really isn't surprising. He was reading the email from his editor again when his cell rang.

"Hi, Mom. How are you?" he asked.

"I'm fine. Why are you at home?"

"So I could answer your phone call."

"It's nice to talk to you, but shouldn't you be out on a date?"

"We're not going to have this discussion again," Harrison said.

"Why? Have you met someone special?"

"No."

"Then we will most definitely be having this discussion again."

"Mom, I'm thirty-five years old. My career requires that I travel a great deal. I'm not in the market for a mate."

"Yes, you keep telling me that. I get it, but you don't even go out with friends. I worry that you're becoming a recluse, Harrison. It's not healthy."

"Sorry to worry you, Mom. I'm fine. I've got to get ready for a trip."

"You're taking a vacation? That's great."

"No, Mom. It's a work assignment. I'll only be gone a couple of days. I'll check in when I get back."

Harrison spent some time reviewing the latest news on EARS before closing his laptop and packing it. Living on an island near Seattle meant he needed to catch the last ferry and get a hotel near the airport to make his early morning flight.

Throwing his bag in the back seat, Harrison drove to the ferry. There hadn't been time for dinner, a hot dog and nachos from the snack bar on the ferry would have to do.

When the ferry docked in Seattle, he hailed a cab and headed for the hotel. After a quick email check, he fell into bed wondering if maybe his mother was right. Maybe it was time to start thinking about a more traditional lifestyle for the future.

CHAPTER SIX

It was a three-hour drive to the observatory, so Erin left early, and made a few stops along the way for coffee, snacks, and a breakfast burrito. She stopped for gas in her hometown west of Boise, before heading out on the last leg of the journey.

When she walked into the convenience store, she recognized the face behind the counter. "Hey, Erin," Mr. Grady said. "Are you here to visit your folks?"

"Not right now," she said, as she picked up a couple bottles of water and a granola bar. She planned to grab lunch at the observatory's snack bar after the press conference, but these things never ran on time, so she wanted to be prepared. "I'm heading out to EARS for a press conference."

"Must be a big deal. A lot of my customers today said that's where they're going. Is this about the call from ET?"

"Yeah. Maybe we'll find out if there's any truth to the rumors."

"Are you broadcasting it?"

"Not live. I'll record it. It should make it on the 5:30 news unless they run really late."

"I'll be sure to tune in. Stop by on your way back to let me know if I need to start wearing my tinfoil hat. OK?"

"Sure, Mr. Grady. I'll let you know if there's anything to worry about."

Back on the road, Erin ran through the questions she would ask if she got the chance. Of course, it would all depend on what information EARS shared in their announcement.

EARS has the big dish antennas like the ones in the movie Contact. The site is remote, but it's impressive when you round the last corner and see all the antennas sitting on the desert floor.

Erin was surprised to see a military vehicle blocking the road in front of her. She wondered if they were turning away everyone except the press that had invites. As she rolled down her window, she counted four armed guards--one on each shoulder of the road and two in the middle beside the truck.

"Hello. I'm here for the press conference," she said, pulling her press credentials from the cup holder and sticking them out the window.

"I'm sorry, ma'am. The press conference has been canceled," the guard said.

"It would have been nice to notify folks before they drove hours to get here. I'll just go to the snack bar then. I need a coffee for the drive back."

Something about this situation had her reporter hackles up.

"I'm sorry, ma'am. You need to leave. This facility is on a security lock down."

"Lock down? This isn't a high security site. They have a snack bar and a gift shop. They give public tours."

"Not today they don't. If you don't leave the property immediately, you'll be arrested."

"What is your name?" she asked as she checked his uniform for a name tag. It looked like standard issue military, but it had no insignia of any kind. No indication of rank. No name. Nothing.

The guard stepped away from her car window and motioned for her to turn around. Two more vehicles had queued up behind her. She did as instructed but pulled over to the side of the road after going only a few yards. She pulled out her phone to film the roadblock.

She moved slowly back toward the guards as they spoke with the driver of the car behind her. She could only hear part of their words. Intent on listening and filming, Erin didn't realize one of the guards had come up beside her until he took hold of her arm.

"Hand over your phone, ma'am," he said.

"I don't think so," she said as he dragged her closer to where one of the other soldiers was speaking to the next driver. It sounded like the driver was getting the same explanation Erin was given. The soldier reached for Erin's phone, but she tucked it into her pocket.

"It's not safe for a woman to drive these deserted roads alone," she said. "Surely you wouldn't want to endanger a citizen."

"She was filming," the guard said, interrupting the conversation between the other guard and the next driver.

"I'm sorry, ma'am. You'll have to hand over your phone. It's a matter of national security."

"You have no right to take the property of a private citizen," she said, turning to look at the man in the next car.

He just shrugged his shoulders. "Are you headed back to Boise?" he asked.

"Yes."

"Great. Give them your phone. I'm heading the same way. I can follow you. If you run into any trouble, I can use my phone to call for help."

"Thanks," she said, giving the helpful man a look that removed any thoughts he might have had about her appreciating him coming to her rescue.

"Thank you, sir. Ma'am, please hand over your phone."

Erin pulled the phone from her pocket and handed it over.

"My name's Harrison Todd," the other driver said. "Just turn on your flashers or pull off the road, and I'll stop."

The helpful Mr. Todd turned his car around and followed as Erin walked back to her car as slowly as she possibly could.

CHAPTER SEVEN

Harrison was surprised when he saw the road blocked and the guards armed with automatic weapons. He assumed the woman in the car in front of him was another reporter who had come to EARS for the press conference. He rolled down his window and listened as the guards talked to her.

Careful to keep his phone below the dashboard, he raised it just high enough for the camera lens to record what was going on in front of him. When the driver ahead turned around, Harrison put the phone out of sight in his bag before pulling up to the guards.

They explained that the site was on a security lockdown. They could not release any information and did not know if the press conference would be rescheduled. Harrison took a close look at their uniforms which looked generically military, but the details were wrong. There was no insignia in view. If they were in the US military, they had taken precautions to hide the details of what branch of the service they were with as well as their names. EARS is privately owned so Harrison doubted these guards were government troops.

When he got back in cell range, he would reach out to some of his contacts and see if he could get a lead on what was going on at EARS. It could be something as routine as a bomb threat that caused them to close the site to public access and cancel the press conference. It could be that simple, but then law enforcement would have handled it not the military or people pretending to be military.

Harrison was ready to turn his car around when the guard walked up pulling the woman from the previous car along with him. They were beside the car, so he couldn't turn around until they moved. They'd caught her filming and wanted to confiscate her phone. She made the argument that it wouldn't be safe to drive back to the city without a cell phone.

It was a pretty flimsy argument since there was no cell service since leaving the small town with a gas station an hour or so earlier.

Harrison was hoping he could talk to the woman and compare notes. She might be a local that could provide insights he wouldn't have. He had to admit he also felt the need to resolve the situation between her and the guards. She was a petite young woman with a gymnast's build. She was barely five feet tall and probably didn't weigh 100 pounds. Her dark brown hair was cut short and stuck up around her head. Seeing this pixie with the pit bull attitude facing off with the armed guards had him feeling the need to protect her though he suspected she didn't feel she needed protection from anyone.

Harrison waited patiently as she got back into her car and pulled out onto the road. When they were out of sight of the roadblock, she picked up speed. He really didn't expect her to need any help, but he intended to follow her until she stopped so they could talk.

Social media would be lighting up with speculation about what was going on at EARS once everyone was back in cell range. As Harrison thought about the situation, that was another aspect that made no sense. He couldn't figure out what could have happened at the observatory that would be worth canceling a scheduled news conference and pissing off a lot of reporters. EARS management had to know they would be criticized on every media platform.

Erin didn't stop until they were back in the small town that had the closest gas station to EARS. She pulled in and parked in front of the convenience store. He pulled in beside her.

CHAPTER EIGHT

"I'm fine. You don't need to keep following me," she said as Mr. Helpful walked around his car and opened her door.

"I'm a reporter for Science Discovery Magazine."

"You can go. I don't need a chaperon."

"I didn't catch your name," he said.

"I didn't throw it. Look, I'm not having a good day. I'm not really in the mood to make new friends."

"Would you be more interested if I told you I have video of the road block."

"Of course, you do, and yet, they didn't seem inclined to confiscate your phone."

"They didn't see me recording, and I hid my phone before I pulled up to the guard."

"Telling me it's my own damn fault really isn't the way to get in my good graces."

"What is the way?"

She glared at him. "Go home or back to the airport or wherever it is you're headed. Thanks for stepping in to keep me from getting arrested."

"You're welcome. I'd like to sit down and discuss what happened out there with you. Are you from Boise?"

"Yeah, but I have a stop to make before I head home."

"I'm staying out near the airport. Is there someplace we could meet for dinner?"

"Since I can't give you my number, I'll pick you up at 6:30."

Erin was surprised he suggested dinner, but if he was a reporter for Science Discovery Magazine, he might have connections that could explain the reason for the lock down at EARS.

He wrote down his hotel and cell number.

"I guess I'll be picking up a new phone when I get back into town," she said.

"I'm going to the hotel and reach out to some of my sources to see if there's any chatter about what's going on at EARS. I'll see you tonight."

He started for his car but changed direction and put his hand on her shoulder when she reached for the door.

"I'm sorry. I still don't know your name."

"Sorry. I'm Erin Mason. I'm a reporter for Channel 8 in Boise."

"Great. I'll see you later," he said and headed for his car.

"Who's your friend?" Mr. Grady asked when she walked in.

"A fellow reporter I met out at EARS," Erin said. "I call him Mr. Helpful."

"That's nice. What was their big announcement?"

"I have no idea. The press conference was canceled."

XXX

When Erin drove into her folk's driveway, her mom came out the door before Erin even got out of the car. "Erin, I'm so glad you came. How are you?"

"Mom, I just talked to you yesterday," Erin said after she was released from a hug. "How's Dad?"

"He's fine. He said to tell you hi and invite you to stay for dinner."

Without thinking, she said, "I can't. I have plans."

"A date?" her mom asked. The look on her face was so hopeful, Erin couldn't disappoint her.

"Yes. I have a date."

"Tell me about him. Is it someone from work?"

"He's a reporter, but he's only in town for a few days."

"Well, plans can change," she said hopefully. "What was the exciting news they announced this morning at the observatory?"

"Let's go inside. I'll tell you all about it if you've got coffee."

"Coffee and fresh-baked banana bread."

Erin followed her into the kitchen and headed to the coffee pot. "You want coffee?"

"I've got tea. Thanks," her mom said. "Tell me about EARS and about your date."

CHAPTER NINE

Harrison picked up a coffee on his way through the hotel lobby. In his room, he pulled out his phone and called his editor. Joyce didn't have any info but said she would let him know if she heard anything. She agreed it was worth poking around a bit while he was in the area to see what he could learn.

He put out some feelers to other contacts he thought might have heard something about what was going on at EARS. Pulling out his cell, he watched the video. A little digging on line confirmed what he suspected, the uniforms looked military but were not used by any branch of the United States armed services. Harrison's brain quickly settled on two reasons why an armed private security force would have locked down EARS. Either that private security force had taken over EARS for some reason, or the people behind EARS had brought in a private security firm to handle some situation that required them to keep everyone out. Neither option was pleasant to consider or seemed likely at an observatory.

Next, he searched for Erin Mason. Ms. Mason had been a reporter for a local television station since she got her journalism degree from Boise State.

By the time he stepped into the shower, he knew a lot about Ms. Mason and yet none of what he read would have led him to believe she was the type to get aggressive when facing down armed soldiers. The on-air pieces she did were the lower level stuff. Harrison laughed aloud at her report on a stolen car carrying exotic animals. The circumstances were amusing, but Ms. Mason seemed to take her job as a journalist quite seriously. According to her bio, she was born and raised in the small town they stopped in on their way back to Boise. That was good. She should have some knowledge of EARS and might even know someone who worked there. All of the science staff lived on site, but the cleaning crew and maintenance people were hired from the local area.

He wasn't sure what he planned to do next about EARS, but his reporter instincts were telling him there was a big story there, and he intended to ferret it out. While he was doing that, he would get better acquainted with Ms. Mason. She was the most interesting woman he'd met in quite some time.

CHAPTER TEN

Erin stopped at home to change into jeans and a more casual shirt and shoes and called Jon. After explaining what happened at EARS, Jon said, "The lockdown is the story now then. Are you coming in to put that together?"

"I'd rather hold off. They confiscated my phone, so I don't have any footage, but there was another reporter there that might have filmed it. I'm going to track him down to see if he's willing to share."

"OK, but we need this on air tomorrow. Sorry about your phone."

"I'm going to pick one up tonight. I'll see you tomorrow."

She grabbed her purse and headed out. It didn't take long to get her new phone in working order but the need to do it pissed her off. She was sure the guy at the phone store was sorry he ever asked if he could help her.

When she got into her car, she called Harrison Todd. "Hello, Mr. Todd. This is Erin Mason. I've got a new phone and am on my way to pick you up for dinner."

"Hello Erin. Please call me Harrison. I'm glad you have a working phone now, but I'm sad you'll no longer require my services as an escort."

This guy is too smooth and too good looking, Erin thought. Although she let her mom believe she was going on a date, the truth was she hadn't been on a date for months. She found all the disappointment not worth the time and effort. Her focus was on figuring out what to do about her career. When she took the job at Channel 8, it was a starting point. She hoped by now she'd have an anchor spot at least for the weekend news shows. Unfortunately, every time a slot opened up, she applied but wasn't selected. Her performance reviews and ratings were always good. They always said she wasn't the best fit. When every person hired over her was a tall, leggy blond, she realized she was never going to be a good fit. The question was whether or not she could find any place that didn't have the same bias. She hated the thought of starting at the bottom again but knew that was likely what she'd have to do.

Between the canceled press conference, losing her phone, and all this self-analysis, Erin really wasn't in a great mood to socialize with a stranger. Before she could get out of the car, Harrison walked out the hotel door and climbed into the passenger side.

"Thanks for picking me up," he said. "Where are we headed?"

After some discussion about food likes and dislikes, they settled on a small Italian restaurant that had a quieter atmosphere where they could talk without having to shout.

They made small talk until they placed their orders, then got down to talking about what happened at EARS. "Why would they invite a bunch of reporters for a press conference then lock the place down?" Erin asked. "It doesn't make any sense."

"I agree," Harrison said. " The men at the gate weren't US military. They had no insignia, and the uniforms weren't standard issue for any branch I know of."

"Then who were they?"

"Private security would be my guess. I came up with a couple of possibilities to explain what happened, but neither is very pleasant to consider." He turned his attention back to his food.

"I'm a reporter. You can't leave me hanging like that. What are these two theories of yours?"

"Either someone has taken over EARS or the observatory called in private security because they have a major problem they need to contain."

"If you think the observatory could have been taken over by some outside force, don't we need to tell someone?"

"I thought about that. We don't have any proof. I'm not sure the authorities would believe us."

"You have your video. They could at least figure out that those soldiers weren't legitimate."

"Do you have any friends in local law enforcement we could talk to?"

At some point Harrison Todd must have done some reporting that wasn't just covering the science beat. She could tell from the way he looked at her that he knew every reporter had a local law enforcement source. "Yeah, I do, but it's a little complicated."

"It always is."

CHAPTER ELEVEN

"Do you have to work tomorrow?" Harrison asked as they were finishing dinner.

"Yeah. My producer wants to run a story about the lockdown," Erin said. "I was hoping maybe we could use some of the footage you shot."

"Sure. I can email you a copy of the video, but I'm not sure we want to push this until we get a better idea what's behind it."

"I disagree. If you think there's even a small chance that an armed force has taken over EARS, then we need to go straight to the police next. Even if it's out of their jurisdiction, they'll have contacts in Oregon they can work with."

"How good a friend is your contact on the force?" he asked. She seemed hesitant to answer. "Is it someone we can layout the facts for and see what they recommend?"

She hesitated again before saying, "Sure, we can do that." She pulled out her phone and sent a text. The answer came as they were walking to the car.

"We can talk to him right now," she said, reading the text before starting the car.

"Great.

Erin didn't say much as they drove through the residential sections of Boise. After a few minutes, she pulled to the curb in front of a small craftsman style house. "Look, he can probably have someone check out our story, but he's a by-the-book, letter-of-the law kind of guy."

"Good to know." Harrison followed her up the steps to the front door and waited while she rang the bell.

The door was opened by a guy about Harrison's age in jeans and a t-shirt. "Hi, Erin. Who's you're friend?"

"I'm Harrison Todd. I'm a reporter for Science Discovery Magazine."

"This is Detective Caleb Murray of the Boise PD."

The two men shook hands and Caleb led them into a small living room and motioned for them to sit.

"OK, Erin, tell me what it is you need my help with this time."

Harrison could tell there was history between Erin and the detective. He couldn't tell if it was personal or professional. "Detective, Ms. Mason and I were both invited to the EARS Observatory today for a press conference. I'm sure there were several other reporters invited as well. Have you heard the rumors that the observatory picked up an alien signal a few weeks ago?"

"Sure. You think they were going to confirm that today?"

"We don't know," Erin jumped in. "I think it was more likely they were going to try to deflect the rumors, but that's really not the issue now."

"Even though they set up this press conference and invited the media, when we reached the site, the road was blocked and there were armed guards turning people away."

"Isn't EARS open to the public?" he asked, directing his question to Erin.

"Yeah. They offer tours every day."

"So, these guards weren't just checking credentials for the press conference?" Caleb asked.

"No. They told me the site was on lockdown and made me turn around."

Erin got into telling her story, and Harrison let her run with it.

"Harrison was in the car behind me in line. There were a couple of others behind him. After I turned around, I pulled over and got out of the car to get some video of the roadblock for my story."

Caleb looked at her and shook his head. "You didn't think they'd have a problem with that?"

"I thought people needed to know something was going on out there."

The tension in the room was rising, and Harrison wanted to smooth things over if he could, so he took up the story and planned to gloss over Erin's encounter with the guards.

"We're hoping maybe you can contact the law enforcement people responsible for that area and have them check on the situation."

Harrison hoped that would be enough, but Erin was too wound up to let it go at that.

"When they saw me filming, one of the guards pulled me back over to the roadblock and took my phone. I told him he had no legal right to do that, but he did it anyway. I told them it wasn't safe for me to drive back without a way to call for help."

"I saw what was going on and didn't want the situation to escalate," Harrison explained. "I offered to follow Erin back to the city in case she ran into any trouble."

The look Caleb gave Harrison as he paced around the room made it clear he didn't believe the science reporter's motives were that impersonal. He stopped in front of Erin.

"I assume you got a new phone, since you called me earlier."

She nodded. "All we want you to do is have someone verify that EARS is on lockdown and find out why if you can," Erin said.

"I'll do some checking and let you know what I find out, but you need to stay out of this," he said. "If something is going on out there, it could be dangerous."

"Harrison, show him..." Before Erin could finish, Harrison stepped between her and Caleb and stuck out his hand.

"Thanks for your help, Detective. We appreciate it. Erin, we should get going." Erin followed his lead but gave him a look that said he'd have some 'splainin' to do when they got in the car.

CHAPTER TWELVE

Erin knew Caleb would help her. Even when he thought she was chasing a lead she should leave alone, he always helped as long as he could do so without crossing that big, wide ethical line he drew in the sand to protect his career when they first started dating.

Back in the car, she turned to Harrison. "Care to tell me what that was all about?"

"What?" he asked, trying to play innocent.

"Why didn't you want me to mention the video? If you showed that to Caleb, he'd be calling in the cavalry right now." As soon as the words were out of her mouth, she understood why he did it. "You think there's a story at EARS. Maybe it's not the story the press conference was supposed to give us, but it's something big."

"What's the story with you and Caleb?" he asked.

"Just typical cop reporter antagonism," she said, hoping to deflect his questions. Harrison Todd was a very good reporter. He didn't miss much, and Erin suspected he sensed she and Caleb shared history. They'd been engaged until Erin realized she loved everything about Caleb, but she didn't love Caleb.

"What next?" she asked as she pulled into the parking lot of his hotel.

"Let's meet for lunch tomorrow. I should have some more information by then," he said, getting out of the car. "Thanks for all your help today."

"You too," she said.

"I'll pick you up at the station tomorrow," he said, waving before walking through the hotel's front door.

Erin sat there for a couple of minutes thinking about Harrison Todd. Despite his protective streak, she was attracted to him. Tonight's dinner had been the best first date she had in a while.

"Stop it," she reminded herself. *This is work. It wasn't a date. It was about the story.*

XXX

Driving to work the next morning, she tried to figure out how to handle Jon. He would want to put something out about the canceled press conference. Other news outlets would be doing that.

On her desk was a sticky note that said, "Jon's office," so she dropped her stuff into her chair and walked down the hall. Jon was on the phone when she walked in, but he motioned her to a chair.

It took some negotiating, but he agreed to let her handle it her way for now. She rounded up Trey and recorded the segment in one of the small sound stages.

"Yesterday morning, I drove out to the EARS observatory to attend a press conference. Reporters from several local and national media outlets received invitations.

"We were expecting EARS management to either admit they picked up a signal that they were still validating or deny they recorded anything of interest.

"What I didn't expect was to be turned away at the entrance. I grew up not far from EARS and have taken a tour of the facility as I'm sure many of you have done with your families.

"The press conference was canceled without notice leaving us to wonder if EARS simply scheduled the announcement before they were ready. For now, all we have is speculation. Once we can verify why the press conference was canceled, we'll share that with the Channel 8 audience."

Once the segment was ready to go, Erin headed out to meet Harrison for lunch.

XXX

"The only way to find out what's going on at EARS is to get into the observatory," Harrison said.

"I agree, but I don't think that's likely with all the guards."

"I found a way in," he said.

"OK."

"How are your climbing skills?"

"Great. I grew up around here," she said. That was true, but the last thing she climbed was out her bedroom window and into the back of Chad Young's pickup truck when she was in high school. Harrison Todd didn't need to know that.

Obviously rational thought had escaped her, because she agreed to join Harrison on an expedition to scale a rockface that would lead them onto the backside of EARS property.

"Do you have climbing gear?"

"Sure," she said.

They talked about timing and agreed to get an early start in the morning. "Text me a list of the gear we need. We can meet at the convenience store where we stopped on the way back from EARS. Will that work?"

CHAPTER THIRTEEN

EARS lab director Belinda Jenkins stressed the party line of how important it was to keep a lid on the problems with the animals. "This is a critical time for EARS. We can't let your work jeopardize what's going on with the observatory, Dr. Young."

"I think the best way to keep this quiet is for us to round up the escaped animals before they can hurt anyone or be seen by the public," Chad said. "Give me two security guards. We'll track the animals down and tranquilize them. Once we have an animal sedated, I'll call and give transport the location."

Director Jenkins didn't say anything for a few minutes. She really didn't have any other options. They needed to capture the animals as quickly as possible. In the end, the director approved Chad's plan and by afternoon he had two guards assigned to help him round up the escaped creatures.

XXX

Hastings International owns hundreds of acres around the complex, but it isn't fenced. It's a remote site surrounded by wilderness. There was no guarantee the bears or cats hadn't wandered outside the boundaries of EARS.

The three hunters headed out at daylight. Both guards had military experience, and Chad did what he could to educate them about the risks the animals posed. Only time would tell whether or not they were paying attention.

When they took a break for lunch, one of the guards, Darnell, wandered into the brush for a bathroom break.

Chad dropped his sandwich, when he heard Darnell scream. He grabbed his rifle and headed into the brush. A pack of scimitars were attacking Darnell. Chad took one look at the collar of red tissue and exposed bone where the man's neck should be and knew Darnell was already dead.

Stokes came up behind him, but one look at the body had him bent over vomiting. Two of the cats were fighting over Darnell's body while two more turned their attention to Chad and Stokes. Chad fired at the nearest cat. He hit it, but it didn't go down, so he fired a second tranquilizer round into it. It charged him but fell over a few feet short of its target. Stokes had his riffle up, but before he could fire, one of the cats plowed into him knocking him off his feet.

Stokes fought to get his gun in position and fired a dart into the animal's neck. Chad got a dart into the cat too, but it still didn't fall. These were big animals, and it took a while for the drugs to take effect. The cat was still attacking Stokes, so Chad turned his rifle around and swung for the fences like he was in the World Series. The stock of the rifle hit the back of the cat's head, and the creature dropped to the ground unconscious.

The other two cats were feasting on Darnell, so Chad helped Stokes to his feet and moved away as quickly as the man's injuries allowed. They were leaving a trail of blood, but there was nothing to do about that. Once they put some distance between them and the cats, Chad pulled out his radio. "We tranquilized two Homotheriums. They're only a few feet apart. There are two others in the area so be prepared." He gave them the location and put the radio away.

Chad helped Stokes to some rocks where they both had a good view back the way they came. "Can you shoot if you need to?"

"Think so," Stokes said. Both of his arms were bloody from the attack. He'd been holding them at his throat trying to protect himself. Chad leaned his gun against the rocks and shrugged out of his pack. He dug out the first aid kit, cleaned and bandaged Stokes' wounds, and handed the guard some ibuprofen. Chad put the kit back in his pack and picked up his radio again.

"This is Dr. Young. I need medev..."

Stokes put his hand on Chad's arm. "I'm OK. Let's keep going."

The two remaining hunters moved out but stayed on high alert. They stopped every 30 minutes to drink water and give Chad a chance to evaluate whether or not he needed to call a medevac for Stokes.

They found some bear scat, but the sandy soil made it difficult to track anything. There were few places where tracks could be seen. "Stokes, I think we need to change tactics," Chad said, as he pulled out the map. "The only place we're likely to find prints is where there's moisture. The animals all need water. Let's head down to the stream and see if we can pick up a trail or find a place to lay an ambush."

There weren't many permanent water sources in the area, but there were arroyos which flowed with water when it rained or during snow melt in the spring. Even in the dry summer heat some of the low areas would have water or at least moisture in the soil.

CHAPTER FOURTEEN

"Are you sure about this?" Joyce asked after Harrison explained his plan for getting into EARS. "If there is something going on, it could be dangerous. Are you sure this woman realizes what she's getting into?"

"She understands. Erin's as committed to getting this story as I am. Look, I know this might turn out to be something outside the magazine's focus area. If that happens, maybe we can find an appropriate outlet for the story once we have it."

"Just be careful," Joyce said. "We'll figure out what to do with the story once we know what this is all about."

After talking with Joyce, Harrison worried that maybe he shouldn't have involved Erin in his plan. *She seems like a nice girl-a girl I could enjoy getting to know better but putting her in danger probably wasn't a good way to start a relationship,* Harrison thought.

"Crap, where did that thought come from." He tried to wrap his head around the idea that he was personally interested in Erin. Once he accepted that, he had to be sure he could keep her safe if they were putting themselves in harm's way. Harrison spent the morning putting things in place to help him accomplish that.

He pulled into the convenience store and filled up with gas, while he waited for Erin. She pulled in when he was walking out of the store. She rolled down her window when he walked up. "Just follow me to my folks," she said. "We can leave one of the cars there."

"Great."

Harrison followed Erin a couple of blocks before she pulled up in the driveway of a small ranch home. She walked up to his window. "Do you want to drive?"

"Yeah. Let's transfer your stuff," he said, climbing out. "Do you need to go in?"

"No, but Mom will be out any minute to check you out."

"OK. Anything I should know?"

"Just smile and endure." She parked her car, and they started moving gear from her car to his rental SUV. They were nearly finished when an older woman walked down the front steps.

"Are you sure you don't want to come in for coffee or a bite to eat?" she asked.

Harrison pasted on what he hoped was his most charming smile and walked over to her. "Hello Mrs. Mason," he said, holding out his hand and shaking hers. "I'm Harrison Todd. It's nice to meet you. We're in a bit of a rush this morning, so we'll just have to come back another time to take you up on your kind offer."

Erin's eye roll said he was probably laying it on a little too thick, but it seemed to have the desired effect.

"You kids stay safe. Come in for coffee if you have time when you stop by for Erin's car."

"Thanks, Mom," Erin said, walking over to give the woman a hug.

"It was nice to meet you, Mrs. Mason," he said as he opened the passenger door and waited for Erin to get settled before closing it and walking around to climb behind the wheel.

CHAPTER FIFTEEN

Erin should have been happy that Harrison charmed her mom, but somehow it pissed her off a little bit. "What was all that with my mom?" she asked as they headed toward EARS.

"I smiled and did better than just endure," he said. "I think she likes me."

"It seemed that way, but now she'll think we're dating."

"What's so wrong with that idea?" he asked.

What could she say? "You live in Seattle, right?"

"Yes, but I travel a lot for work."

"That could be a problem," she said.

"Why? I didn't peg you as the clingy, needy type."

"I'm not, but sometimes you just want to... Wait. Why are we even discussing this?"

She tried to hide her frustration with the topic but could tell by his smile that he knew she was interested. "What's the plan for this secret mission?" she asked, hoping to get the conversation back on firmer ground.

He explained where to turn off the highway after they passed the entrance road for EARS. They debated driving down the access road far enough to confirm whether the roadblock was still in place but decided against it. Harrison thought it might put the guards on alert if they saw a car drive in and turn around.

"Do you do a lot of this kind of stuff?" she asked as they were pulling gear out of Harrison's rental SUV.

"What? Hiking?"

"Yeah or climbing?"

"When I can," he said. "I haven't done much rock climbing this year. What about you?"

"The same. Work has been crazy for a while. I'm considering looking for another job. I've been at the station long enough to know they're never going to give me an anchor spot. I don't have the look they want." she said, adding air quotes around the word look.

"Then they're crazy," he said, dragging his eyes over her from toe to head.

With their packs loaded with gear, they started up the trail. "If we meet anyone, just follow my lead," he said. "We've got about an hour's hike before we come to the cliff face."

Harrison seemed to want to talk while they walked, but Erin found it difficult to do that and keep breathing. Most of her running was done on a treadmill at the gym. This hike was mostly uphill which seemed to require a lot more energy. She thought if she could keep him talking, she could concentrate on breathing.

"Does anyone call you Harry?"

"Only family and not if they want to stay on my good side," he said.

"So you do have a good side?" she joked. "Nice to know. How did you go from astronomer to reporter? Those fields seem pretty different."

"I grew up in Montana," he said. "The big sky nickname sucked me in. I grew up watching the stars. I loved studying astronomy but looking for a job showed me just how limited my options were. I always enjoyed writing, so I found the perfect way to combine the two."

"You don't have dreams of being the first to discover some heavenly body?"

Turning to face her, he said, "I'd say I'm doing a good job of that." That earned him another eye roll.

He stopped when they reached a wall of rock that went straight up. He checked his GPS. "This is it. This is the border of EARS property."

"You can't really expect to climb that," she said, looking up. To her, it looked like it went straight up at least a thousand feet.

CHAPTER SIXTEEN

The cliff face was steep, but the rock was soft and well-eroded, so there were plenty of hand and foot holds. "This looks pretty easy. I can free climb this no problem," Harrison said. "Are you OK with that?"

"You mean climb without a rope?"

"It'll be quicker."

"Um. I don't free climb," she said. "I've only ever climbed with a rope and harness." She didn't tell him that was just the night before at the Y's climbing wall.

"That's OK. I'll set a few anchor points for you on the way up." He noticed she looked terrified.

They dumped out the climbing gear and gathered what they needed. He put the rest back in his pack. "When was the last time you climbed?"

"It's been a while," she said, casting an anxious glance to the cliff face.

He grabbed the gear and started to climb. The best places to study the sky are usually places with few humans. Most of Harrison's adult life was spent in remote areas, so he learned to enjoy the outdoors and picked up quite a few skills along the way. He enjoyed climbing, though he hadn't done much of it lately. This was a simple climb without any obvious challenges. When he was about halfway up the wall, he stopped and looked down at Erin. She was watching him, so he smiled hoping that might ease her nerves a bit.

When he got to the top, he shrugged out of his pack and sat down near the cliff's edge. "Come up whenever you're ready." He pulled a bottle of water from his pack, and when he looked over the edge again, Erin was still standing on the ground. "Is something wrong?" he asked.

She turned and gave him a thumbs up sign before walking to the cliff face and clipping the rope to her harness. After the first couple of moves, she stopped. Harrison didn't want to push her, but if she couldn't make the climb they'd have to come up with a different plan. There was a way they could hike in, but it would add an extra ten miles or more to the hike. When she didn't start moving again after a couple of minutes, he called to her again.

"Is there a problem?"

"I'm good," she answered, "just getting back into the movements."

The more he watched her, the more convinced he was that she had never climbed before. It made no sense though. Where did the gear come from?

When she was within reach, Harrison laid flat on his stomach and let her grab his arm so he could help her to the top of the cliff. She collapsed on the ground beside him rolling onto her back. He could see the relief on her face. *This woman should never play poker,* Harrison thought.

"You've never climbed before have you?" he asked as they laid there side by side.

Once she got her breath, she asked, "What gave me away?"

"Everything. So why did you agree to come?"

"I want this story. I'm thinking about quitting channel 8, and I've been thinking it might be time to give up on my dream of a career in journalism. If that's the case, I want to go out with one big story. This is my chance."

Harrison stood up and offered her a hand. They put their packs on, he checked the GPS, and they headed in the direction of the EARS complex.

"Where did you get the gear?" he asked as they walked.

"My brother's friend is a climber."

"And he just loaned you the gear even though he knows you don't climb?"

"He gave me a lesson last night on the climbing wall at the Y."

"And he thought that was good enough?"

"No. He thought that was a date," she said and continued walking. Erin Mason was one determined woman.

CHAPTER SEVENTEEN

Chad and Stokes had been walking along the valley floor for a while before they spotted the first animal signs. Stokes stopped to check it out, and Chad knelt beside him. "Animal, but not the ones we're looking for," Chad said.

A mile or so further along the arroyo, Chad stopped where there were some tracks in the damp soil. "These were made by a short-faced bear."

"How can you be sure it's not just a regular bear?" Stokes asked.

"A normal black bear's front paw measures about five inches. This is at least twice as large. It's got to be one of ours."

They walked along the arroyo looking for more tracks. They found more short-faced bear tracks and were following them. Climbing out of the arroyo the prints were faint but still visible if you looked closely. Once the tracks ran out, they followed the trail by finding broken branches or plants that had been stepped on by something heavy.

"Did you hear that?" Stokes asked as he pulled his rifle up to his shoulder.

"Yeah. There was some sort of low rumble. "I'm not sure what it is. Let's keep moving but be careful."

The two hunters walked a little further, but it was difficult to concentrate with the noise growing louder.

In a flat clearing dotted with low scrub and cactus, Chad stopped to look in the direction of the noise. A cloud of dust was rising into the sky. It took a minute for him to realize what was happening.

"Run for the rocks," Chad yelled, sprinting for some big boulders on the far side of the open area. He squeezed through some spaces between the rocks and climbed up where he could get a better look at what was bearing down on them.

Stokes stood frozen where Chad left him. The noise was so loud, Chad had to fight the urge to put his hands over his ears. Instead, he put both hands around his mouth and shouted, "Stokes, move. Get to the rocks."

He kept yelling--repeating the warning over and over. Finally, Stokes turned his head to look at Chad as a herd of pronghorn antelope ran him over.

When the last antelope passed by, Chad started down to check on Stokes. Before he left the protection of the rocks, he looked in the direction the herd came from. There was another dust cloud coming. Whatever it was, it was coming fast. Chad ran out to drag Stokes to safety. He checked for a pulse, already knowing the man was dead. His body had been flattened.

Chad pulled out his radio, but before he could make the call he was surrounded by wild horses. Somehow, they all went around him, though one or two bumped his shoulders and spun him around causing the radio to fly out of his hand.

He wasn't sure how long he stood there looking after the horses before it hit him that these animals were all running away from something. He had a pretty good idea what might have caused the stampede. Without anymore thinking, he took off running in the same direction as the animals. He veered off and climbed through some brush and up a ridge until he had to stop to catch his breath.

How in the hell did things go so wrong? he wondered. The dust cloud from the stampede faded into the distance as he watched. If something was chasing the antelope and horses, it was probably something he created. He heard movement off to his right. He brought the rifle around in case he needed it, but he didn't see anything. Finding some kind of shelter became his focus. Part of him wanted to run back to the complex as fast as he could, but another part of him didn't want to make a sound for fear it would bring an animal attack.

Eventually his adrenaline waned, and he fell into a calmer rhythm. Although he heard noises in the brush, he never saw anything until he climbed another ridge. Surveying his surroundings, he saw the roof of a cabin in the distance. After taking a few minutes to watch for movement between his current location and the roof, he headed toward what he hoped would be shelter where he could rest and figure out his next move.

CHAPTER EIGHTEEN

"What's the plan?" Erin asked when they stopped for a water break. She was exhausted and hadn't seen any sign of the EARS complex even when they were on higher ground and had a good view of the surroundings.

"I'm hoping when we get within sight of the complex, we'll be able to figure that out."

"That's it?" Erin couldn't believe she'd gone through that climb and all this walking with no real idea what they were going to do.

"It's hard to make a plan without knowing if we can get into the complex or not. We'll have to figure things out as we go."

They walked down into a flat valley. Harrison knelt down and looked closely at the sandy soil. "What's so interesting about sand?" she asked, kneeling beside him.

"A lot of animals have been through here recently. Maybe they lease this land out to ranchers for cattle grazing."

"We should watch where we step," she said, standing up and continuing across the open area to a line of trees at the base of a ridge. She was walking with her head down checking for cow patties, when she saw a print.

"Check this out," she called.

Harrison walked up behind her and knelt to examine the track. He pulled out his phone and took a photo.

"Do you have bears around here?"

"When I was on a bigfoot hunt, they gave me bear spray because there were bears in the area, but we didn't see anything. Is that a bear track? What are you grinning about?"

"I'm just trying to picture you on a bigfoot hunt. How did that go?"

"It was a farce, but I did the story."

"Is that part of why you're thinking about leaving Channel 8?"

"Not just that, but it certainly wasn't the highlight of my journalistic career," she said. "Now can we get back to the print. Do you think a bear made it?"

"I think so, but it's a lot larger than any bear track I've ever seen."

"Great. Something else to worry about."

As they walked, she realized she should have asked a lot more questions about Harrison's plan. She didn't know if they'd be hiking for hours or days. She hadn't even thought about running into wild animals. All of her focus was on what was happening at EARS.

"Any idea how much further we have to walk?" Erin asked when they stopped for another break.

"Not sure," he said, kneeling to look at something on the ground.

Before she could question him further, he walked up and put his finger to her lips. She heard some rustling in the brush but couldn't see anything.

Harrison stepped in front of her and pulled a gun she didn't know he had. Holding the gun in his right hand, he took her hand in his left and moved back slowly pushing her along. He put his lips to her ear. "If I say run, turn around and run until you can't run any further. I'll catch up if I can."

He pointed his gun toward the noise and waited. Erin looked over his shoulder. "It's just a mule deer," she said with an audible sigh of relief.

Harrison lowered the gun. "Sorry. I really hadn't expected there to be so much wildlife out here."

"Then why'd you bring the gun?"

"I needed to be able to protect you."

Erin wasn't usually a fan of the macho protector kind of guy, but in this case, she realized it was good that at least one of them was prepared. "Thanks."

The mule deer sniffed the air and ran off while they stood catching their breath. To shift her focus away from the pain in her legs and feet, she ran some ideas through her head of what might be going on at EARS. Since the day of the press conference, she'd been trying to come up with some explanation that made sense. Her best guess was that they picked up some signal they didn't want to make public until the government was prepared to deal with the fallout of that announcement. She didn't believe the signal was alien. As a seasoned reporter she knew it was much more likely they picked up something from a spy satellite or something. Hastings International was probably cranking up their corporate spin machine to find a way to turn this situation to their advantage.

Harrison was surveying their surroundings when they stopped at the top of a ridge. "Come on," he said, reaching for her hand.

"Are there more animals?"

"Probably, but I saw a roof. I think there's a cabin."

Harrison seemed to think it was a big deal. Erin didn't share his excitement. The idea of getting inside, sitting in a comfortable chair, and drinking a cup of hot coffee sounded great to her, but she figured any cabin that wasn't in ruins would be locked.

Earlier in the day, she thought the uphills would kill her, but she learned that downhill wasn't good either. The real problem was that hiking used muscles Erin hadn't been exercising nearly enough. She was trudging along with her head down, concentrating on putting one foot in front of the other, when she heard a growl.

She pulled her head up and saw a huge animal facing off with Harrison. She screamed for help as it swiped a huge paw across his chest. He pulled out his gun and shot it, but the animal didn't fall over, instead it moved closer and clamped its jaws around Harrison's upper arm.

Just then a man ran out of the cabin with a rifle. He fired his weapon, and the animal yelped and released his grip on Harrison's arm. He turned toward the man who fired another shot, but it missed. The animal ran off.

"Help me get him inside," the man said, shouldering his rifle and bending down to help Harrison.

CHAPTER NINETEEN

Something about that voice sounded familiar to Erin, but she was focused on getting Harrison inside where they would be safe.

"What are you two doing out here?" the man asked as they eased Harrison into a chair.

Erin stood up, dropped her pack on the floor, and looked into a face she hadn't seen in more than a decade. "Chad?"

"Erin? What the hell are you doing here?"

"I was going to ask you the same thing."

Harrison moaned.

"We need to take care of him. Do you have a first aid kit?"

Harrison gritted his teeth and said, "Pack."

She started to help Harrison out of his pack before she saw how much damage there was to his upper arm. "I think we'll have to cut his pack off," she told Chad. "Do you have a knife?"

Chad started opening draws and cabinets looking for something they could use to cut off the pack. Concentrating on their search, they both turned their backs on their patient until they heard something hit the floor. Erin spun around and saw a Swiss army knife lying at her feet. Harrison had managed to get it out of his pocket.

Chad picked up the knife and made quick work of cutting the straps of Harrison's backpack. She set the pack on the table and pulled out the first aid kit.

After assessing Harrison's wounds, they set to work cleaning them. The arm was more serious than the swipes across his chest. Once it was cleaned up, it didn't look quite as bad as Erin originally feared. "Are you OK Erin?" Harrison asked as she worked to bandage his arm.

"I'm fine. Our rescuer here is Chad Young. We went to high school together. Chad this is Harrison Todd."

"Not a great way to meet," Chad said. "What are you two doing out here?"

"We're reporters," she said as they turned their attention to the wound on Harrison's chest. The animal had swiped its claws across his chest leaving an obvious reminder of the creature's size. "Do you know what kind of animal that was?"

There was a time when she could read Chad Young's expressions as well as her own. Something passed across his face that she couldn't interpret before he said, "It was a bear."

"What the hell kind of bears do you have around here?" Harrison asked. "That thing was a giant."

"We need to come up with a plan," Chad said. "Let's see if we can find anything here to eat or drink."

"This isn't your place?" she asked.

"No, but I'm glad it's here."

After giving Harrison some ibuprofen for the pain, Chad and Erin searched the cabin for anything useful. It was one room with a wood stove, but no wood. There were a few cans of beans but little else.

As they dumped the contents of all three packs on the bed, Harrison asked. "What are you doing out here, Chad?"

"I work at EARS."

When Chad didn't offer any more, Erin looked at Harrison and saw that the two of them were on the same page. "What kind of work do you do?" she asked.

"Still a science nerd," he said.

"Look, I'm not sure what's going on, but you and I were friends once. I figure we still are. Harrison and I were invited to a news conference at EARS a few days ago. When we got to the gate, we were turned away by armed guards that told us the press conference was canceled. We're trying to find out what's going on."

"I'm afraid I can't help you with that. I didn't know about the guards."

"What exactly do you do at EARS?" Erin asked.

"I'm a biogeneticist," he answered.

It took a few minutes, but they eventually realized they had to depend on each other to survive. From that point on, Chad was a lot more forthcoming.

"So, you created the bear that attacked Harrison?" she asked.

"I guess," he said. "You won't hold it against me, will you, Harrison?"

"I'm going to reserve my decision until we figure out what's going on. Will someone be coming to rescue you?"

"I'm not sure," Chad said.

They ate protein bars, drank water, and listened to Chad's story about what happened with the animals in the lab beneath EARS.

"Do you think they did record an alien signal?" Erin asked.

"They definitely recorded a signal they didn't expect," Chad said. "Whether or not it came from aliens, I have no idea."

"I know this place isn't very comfortable, but I think we should stay here tonight and make the best of it," she said. "I wouldn't want to be sleeping out there with those creatures around."

They had no way to call anyone for help. The three of them went outside to use the pit toilet behind the cabin. One of them held the tranquilizer rifle and one had Harrison's gun while the other visited the outhouse.

CHAPTER TWENTY

Safely back inside, Harrison took more pain meds and tried to get comfortable on his uninjured side on the lumpy mattress on the cot.

Chad and Erin pulled chairs up to the table and settled in to catch up on their lives since high school. They dated during their junior and senior years. They were both anxious to leave their small hometown behind, but Chad was running further and faster than she was. He got a scholarship to USC and couldn't wait to get to California. They broke up right after graduation and hadn't been in touch since.

The two old friends talked about what they'd done and commiserated over things that hadn't worked out the way they planned. "Why did you create these animals?" she asked. "I can't see any good reason for them."

"I know how it looks. I'm sorry for all the deaths they caused."

"What good reason could there be to have these creatures running around? I just don't get it."

Chad took a while to answer. "You're right. I got caught up in the science. The challenge was to prove I could do it. I lost sight of everything else."

"I can understand that, but why would a company like Hastings International fund your work? What's in it for them?"

He was quiet for a few minutes. "I guess I should have asked more questions, but when Reingold Hastings took a personal interest in my work, I was just happy to be able to continue. I think at some point my hope was that I'd find a way to take what I learned from my work with the animals and apply it to something that would help people--you know like using gene manipulation to overcome a genetic disease. Many medications have an animal origin. It's possible animals that have gone extinct could hold the key to curing modern diseases, but now that I've seen what these animals can do, I'm not sure it's worth the risk. I can't imagine why Hastings would want to reintroduce them."

"How did they get loose?"

His story started with the first attack when the signal was played over the speakers throughout the complex.

"Do you think there's some link between the signal and what's going on with these animals?" Harrison asked.

Chad and I both turned our heads to look his way. He was sitting up on the side of the cot.

"I'm sorry if we woke you," Erin said. "How are you feeling?"

"I'll be OK."

"The signal got them riled up," Chad said, "that's for sure, but I'm not sure that any noise played over and over like that wouldn't have caused the same affect. It was pretty annoying even to us humans."

Chad explained how he came to be out hunting his creations and what happened to the other hunters that were with him.

Harrison broke the silence that had fallen inside the cabin when he said, "I think the animals may be the reason the site was on lockdown. Everyone outside assumed it was related to the signal, and I guess in some way maybe it was, but no one knows about these animals."

Harrison's comments about the lockdown made sense. They'd been struggling to figure out why EARS would have scheduled a press conference about the signal and then canceled it, but Chad's work was secret. No one knew about the lab under EARS. Erin could imagine how the local population would react to knowing someone was creating prehistoric animals in their backyard even if the animals hadn't escaped.

Harrison took some more pain meds and laid down again. Chad and Erin stayed at the table talking.

"How long will it take to get back to the EARS complex?" she asked.

"Depends on how he's doing. I figure it's probably a five-hour hike. It'll be longer if he has to take it slow. We'll have to be prepared for the animals. Do you know how to shoot?"

"Not really. You do remember who I am, right? I'm not really an outdoors person at all, but I'll manage whatever you need me to do tomorrow. How many of those bears are out there?"

"Only two, but the cats are probably the greater threat."

"I'm guessing you don't mean some normal kind of cat like a cougar or a mountain lion."

"Homotheriums," he said. "Their other name is scimitar cat. They died out about 10,000 years ago. They're big. The adults weigh upwards of 600 pounds. Scimitars are fast, and they hunt in a pack."

"They're like the velociraptors of the prehistoric cat world."

"That works. What's the story with you two," Chad asked, nodding toward the cot where Harrison was sleeping.

"Too soon to know," she said. "We just met a few days ago. Why? Are you jealous?"

"Seeing you again does make me wonder why we didn't bother keeping in touch."

CHAPTER TWENTY-ONE

Chad and Erin spread out a space blanket on the floor and leaned on each other. It wasn't comfortable, but at least they were safe from the creatures outside.

Erin woke up when Harrison moaned. When she checked on him, he was sweating, and his skin was really hot to the touch. She gave him another dose of medication and went back to her spot on the floor beside Chad. "He's running a fever," she said. "We need to get him to a doctor."

"Any animal bite is likely to get infected. We'll head out at first light."

When Chad woke her, it was still dark outside. "It'll be light soon," he said. "Let's get ready to go."

Erin woke Harrison, and they ate protein bars, drank water, and checked the weapons. After a stop at the outhouse, Erin and Chad shrugged into their packs and the three of them headed off.

Their route was the fastest way back to the complex with the fewest obstacles. They had no idea if the animals were still in the area, but they were cautious. If any of them heard or saw anything, they stopped until they were sure it was safe to continue. For the first hour, it felt like they were barely making any progress because they stopped so frequently but after that they fell into a rhythm.

"What's the plan once we get to EARS?" Erin asked as they stood around taking a water break.

Neither man answered immediately which worried her.

"I guess we should have thought about that," Harrison said. "I don't see them wanting this story getting out."

"You're right," Chad agreed. "Maybe we need to rethink this."

Erin couldn't believe Hastings International would go so far as to harm them, but the guys weren't convinced.

"Chad, I'm not sure how this will affect your job, but Harrison, you and I can leave the way we came." As she said it, a picture of the cliff face appeared in her head. "Although, maybe with your arm that's not an option."

Lots of discussion brought no clear choices, so they headed toward the cliff face with the vague plan that at least Erin would leave that way. Harrison might join her, and Chad might go as well. If not, she'd get back to the car and get law enforcement involved to search for the two men. She wasn't keen on leaving them and hoped they'd come up with a better plan by the time they reached the cliff.

While they walked, Harrison and Chad speculated about the possibility that the alien signal affected the animals in some way causing them to become more aggressive.

"Have there been any reports of other animal attacks in the area since the signal?" Harrison asked.

"Not that I've heard about," Chad said. "But we hadn't considered the possibility that the signal was the cause of the animal's behavior. I shouldn't have missed that."

"That seems pretty crazy to me," Erin said.

"It is, but you have animals that haven't existed here for thousands of years and a signal that could have come from an alien civilization somewhere out in the cosmos," Harrison said. "It's all a little crazy."

They fell silent again as they listened for any sound that the animals were near. Harrison held up his hand to stop them. "We're not too far from the cliff. The top is pretty open, so we won't want to be exposed longer than necessary. Let's finalize the plans here."

In the end, they decided they would all climb down the cliff face. There was over an hour of hiking between the cliff and the car. It wasn't safe for anyone to do that alone just like it wouldn't be safe to leave anyone to make their way back to the EARS complex alone.

There'd been no sign of the creatures all morning. They hoped the animals had left the area although that raised a whole bunch of new questions to consider. For now, they were happy to have reached the cliff safely. Erin put the harness on, and Harrison explained what she should do. Both men could help lower her to the bottom if she got into trouble.

To convince herself to step off the edge, she pictured the giant bear that attacked Harrison. For her that was the option--stay up there and face the creatures or face her fear of climbing down the cliff face. The cliff won, and she eased herself over the side. After descending only a few feet, she lost sight of Harrison, but could still see Chad who was lying flat on his stomach so he could watch her descent.

About half way down, there was a jerk on the rope. She looked up, and Chad was gone. "Guys, what's going on?" There was no answer. She considered whether she should go up or down. To be honest, she wasn't sure she could move at all, but it didn't seem advisable to just hang there like a piece of bait dangling on a fishing line. Harrison had told her how to lower herself, so she started moving slowly. Her attention kept shifting between the ground coming up to meet her and worry over what was happening up on top. "Guys, what the heck is going on up there?" Crickets. "Someone yell down and let me know you're OK." More crickets. The sound of gunshots above sped up her descent.

Erin was nearly to the bottom of the cliff, when she heard more gunshots. Movement drew her eyes to the left just as something flew off the cliff above. Just when she realized it was

Chad falling, a second body followed. This one was much larger and fur-covered.

It took a minute for her to realize the voice that was screaming was her own. "Harrison, are you OK?"

There was no answer. She debated trying to climb back up to find Harrison, but she was only a few feet from the bottom. When her feet touched the ground, she ran to the pile of bodies. Chad's body was twisted at an impossible angle, and there was a lot of blood.

Lying closer to the cliff face was the body of one of the scimitar cats Chad talked about. She was pretty sure it was dead, but she had no weapons, so she kept her distance. Erin was pacing along the base of the cliff trying to decide what to do when she detected movement above her. She looked up to see Harrison headed down.

"Are you OK?" she yelled.

"Stay quiet," he said.

He was struggling to get down the rope with his injured hand, but she didn't know how to help him. As she walked around, she picked up some stones and put them in her pocket. She figured if an animal attacked, she could throw them at it. She watched Harrison until he neared the bottom, then she hurried over to greet him.

"What happ..."

He leaned in and kissed her, pulling her close with his uninjured arm. Before he pulled away, he whispered, "We need to stay quiet and move fast. We'll talk in the car."

Harrison nudged her forward, and she started walking down the path they followed the day before. It didn't seem right to leave Chad's body just lying there, but they didn't have any other choice. If they needed to stay quiet, she assumed that meant there might be more of those creatures around. She didn't want to do anything to attract their attention.

CHAPTER TWENTY-TWO

Erin couldn't remember ever being so happy to see a parking lot. Harrison's rental SUV was the only car there. He pulled a couple bottles of water and some granola bars from his pack and put them in the console, before putting the packs in the back seat.

He held the driver's door open and handed Erin the keys. His injured arm meant he couldn't drive. She was sure they heard her sigh all the way in Boise, when they closed the car doors.

"What now?" she asked.

"Head back to your folks. We need to figure out a plan before we get there."

When they reached the paved road, she felt the tension in her shoulders relax a little. "How are you feeling?"

"I think the bite is infected. I'll need some antibiotics, but I'll recover. Are you OK?"

"I'm not even sure. I'm scared, upset, shocked, terrified, sad. It's been a lot to deal with."

"You did great out there. We had no idea about those animals, or we never would have gone in without more protection."

"What happened on the cliff?"

"We were waiting for you to get to the bottom. I had my harness on so I could come down next. We didn't hear or see anything before three of those cats attacked him. He fired at them, but I don't know if he hit them or not. None of them collapsed. If I took a shot, I couldn't guarantee it wouldn't hit him. One of the cats backed off, and I fired at it. I hit it, but it wasn't dead. One of the other cats turned away from Chad. I don't know why. I was lining up a shot, when it lunged at him, and they both went over the edge."

"I'm so sorry about all of this. What are we going to do?"

Rather than stopping at her mom's, they drove straight back to Boise. She took Harrison to the emergency room. They agreed to explain that he was attacked by a bear. When they finished at the hospital, they picked up fast food and headed to Erin's apartment.

After eating, they took turns in the shower. "It's too late to figure this out tonight," she said. "We need some sleep."

"I know we need to notify the authorities, but the situation isn't going to change dramatically in a few more hours."

Despite his objections, she settled Harrison in her bed before curling up on the sofa.

XXX

She set her alarm for six expecting that as tired as she was, she might sleep until noon. Instead She woke before the alarm. They had a lot to do. Erin typed a couple of emails but didn't want to send them until she checked with Harrison to make sure he was still in agreement with the plan.

He walked into the kitchen with his hair still wet from the shower. Despite the lines of exhaustion around his eyes, he was a very attractive man. He leaned down and brushed a kiss across her lips as he headed for the coffee pot.

"Good morning, Erin. We need to talk."

She assumed he wanted to talk about their plans to contact the authorities and release the story about what was going on at EARS. He took a seat at the table and set his coffee mug in front of him before reaching for her hands. "I know the last few days have been crazy, and I will admit that facing the possibility of death a time or two might have changed my perspective some. Before we get into the details we need to handle over the next few days, I just want you to know that I'm glad I met you, and

I'd like the chance to get to know you better when things calm down."

Erin was so surprised, she reached for her coffee while she considered her response. "I'm glad I met you too, Harrison. Things have certainly been lively since you inserted yourself into my life. I'd like the chance to get better acquainted too, but I'll be honest. I'm not sure where my future lies at this point."

After another kiss, they put their plan into action--both personally and professionally.

CHAPTER TWENTY-THREE

A week later...

"Are you ready for this?" Harrison asked as they stood backstage at channel 8.

"Let's do this," she said, leaning in for a kiss before they walked out into the interview area of the local morning show. Erin and Harrison had spent the last week giving statements to law enforcement and working with Jon and Joyce to plan the release of their story. They both received a personal call from Reingold Hastings offering amazing jobs at Hastings International if they didn't go public with the story. They discussed the offers but knew they wanted to let the public know what happened to Chad and the others who were killed in the aftermath of EARS' signal find.

"Welcome to the morning show," the host said. "I'm sure our viewers will recognize Channel 8 reporter Erin Mason. Also joining us today is Science Discovery Magazine reporter and astronomer, Harrison Todd. I understand you two have a story to share about the recent rumors of an alien signal being detected at the EARS observatory."

Erin and Harrison shared their story leaving out any of the gory details, but not glossing over the fact that the prehistoric animals killed or injured several people. Harrison talked about the possibility that something in the animal's genetics was triggered by the signal received from space.

"Have the animals all been captured?" the host asked when they finished, "or are there dangerous creatures still running around the Oregon desert?"

"There are always dangerous creatures in the desert, but Hastings International recaptured all the missing creatures," she said.

"Can you tell us anything more about this alien signal?"

"The scientists at EARS are still studying the signal," Harrison said. "It will be some time before they release any details on its age or source."

After the broadcast, Harrison waited in the lobby while Erin went to Jon's office to turn in her resignation. She still wasn't sure where her future was, but she knew it wasn't at channel 8 or probably any on-air job.

"When are you leaving?" she asked Harrison over lunch.

He pulled out an envelope and slid it across the table to her. "What's this?"

"I'm heading home the day after tomorrow. That's a plane ticket. I thought maybe you'd like to come along. You can see my place in Seattle. The island is quiet. It's a great place to figure things out."

"But not a great place to look for a job," she said.

"Not unless you'd like to work with me. The magazine was pleased with our article. I think we make a great team."

She leaned over and kissed him. "I can't argue with that."

ABOUT JO CAREY

Jo Carey grew up in the Midwest but her curiosity and gypsy-spirit has kept her on the move. She's lived in eight US states and spent three years living in Ireland. She has always loved creature movies, so creatures and bugs often show up in her books.

A former information security compliance guru, Jo writes fast-paced, character-driven science fiction stories. Her tales are filled with humor, romance, and sometimes creatures or aliens, or maybe even all of the above. She often builds her stories around a strong female lead character surrounded by plenty of hunky male heroes.

Jo's been under fire on a golf course and climbed out the roof of an elevator in the Netherlands. Life hasn't been boring. Now residing in Texas, setting often plays a huge role in her stories. Jo was intrigued by the League of Planetary Systems, a world her husband, Frank, created for his science fiction books, and she now writes tales set in that world. Jo was bitten by a cat, a fire ant, and a snake, before succumbing to the bite of the writing bug.

Jo hasn't had personal contact with a cryptid or an alien, but it's never too late.

Jo can be reached via e-mail at
elvenindustriespress@gmail.com.
Jo's Amazon Author page:

http://amazon.com/author/jocarey

www.ingramcontent.com/pod-product-compliance
Lightning Source LLC
Chambersburg PA
CBHW020646130626
46552CB00003B/1420